# KING DUDLEY
## and the
# Golden Mystery

story by
# Kamlesh Mistry
art by
## John Mahomet

Published by Kamsbooks.com
www.kamsbooks.com

ISBN: 978-0-9672778-0-6
Library of Congress Control Number: 2012904098

# Acknowledgements

Many thanks to all the people who have helped me. John Mahomet has done an exceptional job in illustrating this book.

Nisha Amin, Diana Pena, Stephanie Pena, and Andee Pena have provided exceptional feedback on King Dudley's adventures, allowing me to reshape the stories to perfection! Nisha has also provided great marketing support.

Surendra Mistry has provided excellent expertise in the website design of www.kamsbooks.com.

Eby Thomas has provided outstanding moral support and marketing support, as well as feedback on my stories and illustrations.

Emily Kanaval, Jeevan Kanaval, Julia Kanaval, and Mathew Kanaval have provided good feedback of King Dudley's works. Emily has also provided great marketing support.

King Dudley series got started because one friend, Imran Qureshi, suggested that I should pursue publishing my stories. Imran, and his children, Salman and Bilal, have reviewed King Dudley's adventures, and provided good feedback.

Norma Hunter, Caillou Hunter, Craig E. Hunter, Lana Zecevic, Sandra Zecevic, Lindsay Steszewski, Isabella Steszewski, and Velma Newton have supported my endeavors, and provided good feedback on King Dudley's works.

I also thank my family, Rita Mistry (spouse), Nima Mistry (daughter), and Shivam Mistry (son). They have provided great ideas and feedback for King Dudley stories and illustrations.

The greatest thanks goes to my parents, Nirmala Mistry and Bhikhu Mistry. I thank them for many blessings and good wishes.

# CONTENTS

# CHAPTER 1

## At Present—An Introduction to Kingsland

Kingsland is a region on earth that not many people know about. Its inhabitants are descendants of sailors who traveled far away from Europe in the early 1500s. To this very day, most people don't know anything about Kingsland, and most people of Kingsland don't really know how much the rest of the world has changed.

Kingsland is a society of many classes and craftsmen, and it also has some of the same great technological advances found in our world, such as plumbing and electricity. Although its people have devised many of the same inventions as the rest of the world, Kingsland has evolved separately, without help from the outside world. In this land, it is common to refer to a person by profession. For example, a brick maker can be referred to as Brickmaker, a pottery maker as Potmaker, and a taxi driver as Taxidriver.

*How can a whole different world exist right within our reach, yet without us knowing?*

Kingsland is on planet earth, all right. However, *it is a world of its own*, and to get to it, it is said that one has to travel through a port into another dimension.

As one might imagine, Kingsland is a land of many small kingdoms. Leelput and Angelsland are two kingdoms within Kingsland. *King Dudley & The Golden Mystery* is a story about the past of these two kingdoms.

## CHAPTER 2

## Return of King Dudley

Leelaput was a kingdom, small in size, but with many people. Like most other kingdoms in Kingsland, Leelaput was a peaceful land, and the people loved their king. King Dudley was a proud king of a happy people, and he was returning home from a hunting trip. The king's team made their way back from the jungle riding on the backs of elephants. The king's mind started to wonder.

*Before I left for the jungle, I made a grand announcement to my people that I would return home with the skin of a tiger. But the hunt was not exactly successful. What will I tell my people? How embarrassing! They will think of me as a coward.*

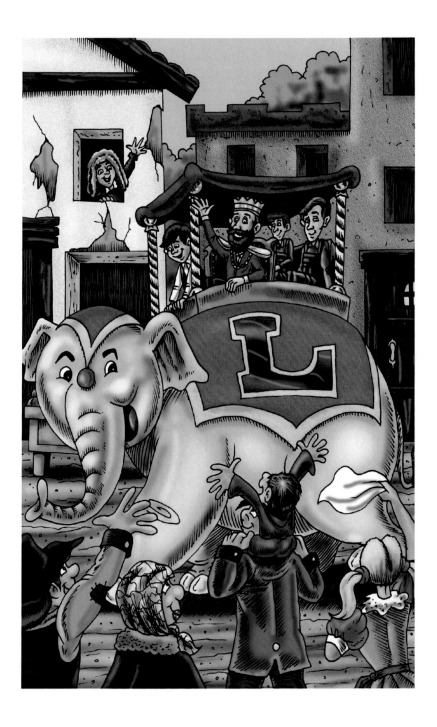

The king's party finally reached Leelaput, and one of the kingdom's guards cleared the way. "Ahoy! Make way. Our beloved king returns!" he exclaimed repeatedly, as he led the king back to his palace.

Most people came out to see their beloved king— Brickmaker, Potmaker, Baker, Baker's wife, and many others. They smiled and waved their hands at the king, his guards, and the ten-year-old prince, Pip, as they rode the elephants back to the palace.

From atop their elephants, they could see the streets behind the main road. There, children were playing hide-and-seek. As the king's team passed through, the smell of delicious, sweet pastries tempted them. Everybody's mouth was watering, but nobody said anything, except Pip.

"Mmmm!" exclaimed Pip. "Father, can we have some cinnamon rolls?"

"Well, if you must, sure. We'll all have some, I suppose," declared King Dudley.

The pastry vendor delivered delicious pastries and hot chocolate. King Dudley, Pip, and the king's guards had a delicious breakfast atop their elephants, as they made their way back home.

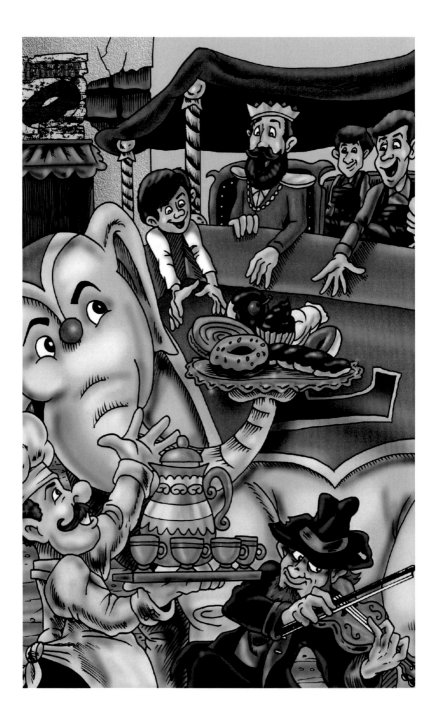

The fiddler's sweet melody of a fast tune echoed at the scene. While moving forward to the next block, the sound of the violin faded away, replaced by a peppy flute player. Musicians made the streets lively, making their living from the passing public.

There were many pedestrians and three-wheeler, battery-powered taxis on the road. However, everyone waited alongside of the road, to let their beloved king through.

Leelaput was a good place to live; taxes were low, people were sociable, food was plentiful, and the basic freedom to think and speak freely was protected by King Dudley's laws. Huge posters could be seen every hundred yards or so. Each poster had a picture of King Dudley, and read: *We love our King!*

He was a friendly and sociable king who conversed freely with his servants and people. As they continued their journey towards the palace, the king's party conversed merrily atop their elephants. The road became less busy as they approached the palace. Brickmaker came out to greet the king. The team stopped for a few minutes while King Dudley chatted with Brickmaker. He was a close friend of the king's family; he was also

a close kin to the queen. Thus, he was more involved with the activities of the royal family.

Smiling, Brickmaker asked, "How was the hunt, Dear Majesty?"

"Oh, fine," replied King Dudley.

"If I'd known you were coming I would have organized a grand party to honor the completion of your tiger hunt."

Embarrassed, the king acknowledged in an uncertain tone, "Yes, that would have been nice." He looked very uncomfortable, and held a fake smile.

"Can I see the tiger?"

The king blushed, and replied, "Why sure, but the body was *too heavy* for all the men, so they are resting by Oyster Creek. They will rest, and arrive late into the night, well past midnight."

"Oh that's great! I can organize a team of fresh, new men, and we can go and get the tiger from Oyster Creek right away, Your Majesty!"

"No, no! That won't be necessary!" the king burst anxiously, "The men want to be left alone to rest! You will not go, and that is an order!"

Pip couldn't help but notice that his father was

becoming increasingly uncomfortable as he spoke one lie to cover another lie; he thought to himself, *Gosh, wouldn't my father have been more comfortable and happy if he just told the truth to begin with?*

"Yes, Your Majesty, we will not go to Oyster Creek. My lady and I will greet them when they arrive late into the night, and we will have refreshments ready for them!"

"Well, the palace isn't much further, and we'll have refreshments for them there!" exclaimed the king.

"That's wonderful! I will come to the palace tonight to visit my dear cousin, Queen Isabella. Then I will be happy to wait for the men and greet them with honor and refreshments!"

The king reacted angrily, "No! You must attend to making more bricks for the palace's new farm house tomorrow, and you must rest! That is an order!"

"Yes, Your Majesty," replied Brickmaker.

The party continued their journey toward the palace, and Pip questioned his father. "Father, you said that we left men behind at Oyster Creek with the tiger, but we didn't. Why did you say that?"

"Our people are expecting a tiger, Pip. We can't

disappoint them and tell them that we didn't bring one back. We made a grand announcement that we would return with a tiger skin before we left for the hunt."

Pip was an inquisitive, intelligent boy. "Why do our people need a tiger skin, and what would happen if you told them what really happened?" asked Pip.

"They might not believe me, and would not think very highly of their king."

Pip nodded his head, but he wasn't very sure of his father's answer.

They continued their journey towards the palace.

"Your Majesty, it is nearing the end of July," said Jordon, one of the king's guards.

*"Why yes, Jordon, it is, isn't it!"* the king declared eagerly. The king's birthday was fast approaching.

"Forty is a special number, perhaps worthy of a grand celebration for our beloved king, Your Majesty," said Jordon.

"Yes, you are quite right. We must start planning," declared the king.

# CHAPTER 3

## The Mysterious Palace of Gold

**O**n the king's fortieth birthday, a grand celebration ensued within the courtyard of the beautiful palace. The palace's open courtyard was conveniently situated in the middle of the castle, and offered constant shade from direct sunlight. From within the courtyard, the various beautiful colors of the palace could be seen. The palace was well-painted in a rainbow of beautiful, light, pastel colors. The celebration was a feast for the eyes, with exotic dancers from various kingdoms, foods and drinks of all kinds, and comedians who wandered about the yard, interacting and cracking jokes with the attendees.

Eventually, the king took center stage and was

receiving complements, gifts, and good wishes from friends. While the party ensued, the king's messenger darted into the gathering, and approached the king with great enthusiasm and excitement.

"Your Majesty! I've news from your friend, King Jaaz!" (*Joz*), exclaimed Messenger.

Messenger was not such a bright fellow, and was far too informal for his title. Nonetheless, he was a perky and lovable guy, and the king had kept him as his messenger, perhaps because somehow Messenger's informality and liveliness were amusing.

From one end of the courtyard to the other, Messenger ran toward the King and repeatedly exclaimed, "He's building a palace of gold, Your Majesty!"

Messenger finally reached center stage, and conversed with King Dudley.

"Calm down!" exclaimed the king.

"Your Majesty, he's building a palace of gold!"

"Who's building a palace of gold?"

"Your friend, King Jaaz, from Angelsland. He's building a palace of gold, Your Majesty!"

"Ha Ha Ha!" scoffed the king, *"King Jaaz*, building

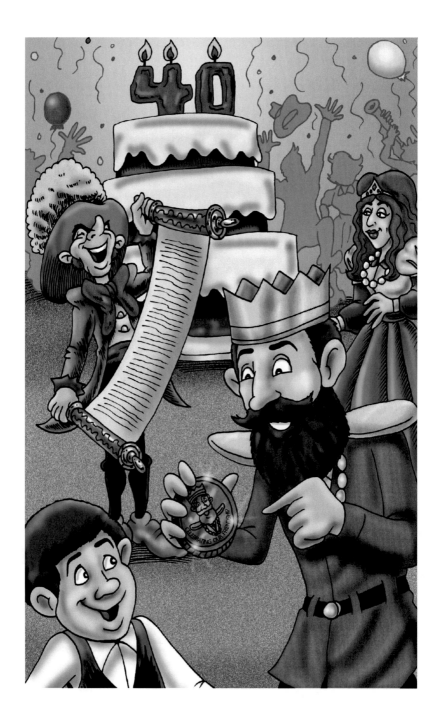

a palace of *gold?* He can't even afford to keep his palace well painted. "

"No, it's true!" exclaimed Messenger, "I saw with my own eyes. He's renovating his entire palace!"

"Well, it's *about time* he painted his palace," the king reasoned, "So you say he's painting it in gold color, aye?"

"No! Gold! He's using real gold!"

Finally, Messenger opened up the letter from King Jaaz, and read it to King Dudley.

> "Dear Friend King Dudley: I'm very sorry I can't make your Fortieth birthday party celebration. My palace is undergoing renovation, so I can't come. But please accept my small gift as a token of our friendship."

"Where's the gift?" asked King Dudley.

Messenger finally took out the gift. It was a friendship medallion with a picture of King Dudley on one side, and King Jaaz on the other. Engraved on the medallion were the words: *Celebrating our Friendship.*

The medallion was thick, heavy, and made of solid gold!

"You say he is making a *palace of gold?*" asked the king.

"Yes, Your Majesty. And Angelsland now looks so different! All the roads are made of cobblestone, and they are even making gardens and a waterpark!"

The king commenced a plan to visit his friend, King Jaaz, to witness the new Angelsland for himself.

# CHAPTER 4

## Off to Angelsland

King Dudley took out his elephant, Shirley, from the barn. He was fond of his elephant, and did not usually go anywhere without her.

"We've got a long trip ahead of us, Shirley," he said, "But I know you can do it, because you've never let me down." He patted her big tummy, and she trumpeted delightfully.

Angelsland was a kingdom to the north of Leelaput. King Dudley, his comrades, and Pip set off on the backs of elephants to meet King Jaaz.

After a long journey, they arrived at the gate of Angelsland and were greeted very warmly by the kingdom's guards, because they recognized that King Dudley was a good friend of King Jaaz. James, one of

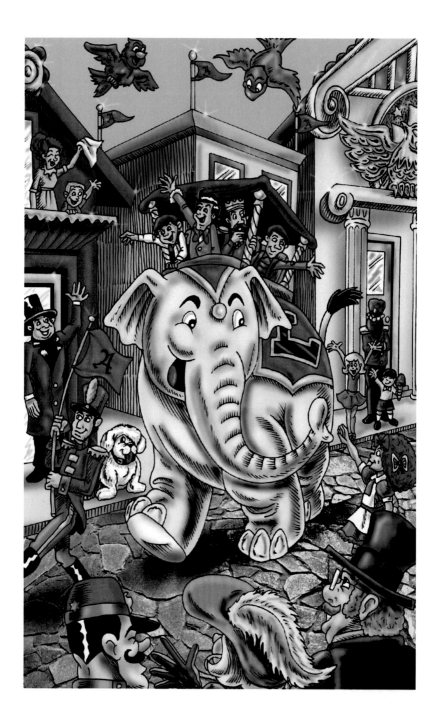

the guards, climbed atop the king's elephant, Shirley. He personally escorted them to King Jaaz's Palace, while another guard led the way, clearing the road.

"Ahoy! Make way for our king's friend, and our friend, King Dudley!" announced the lead guard, as they lead King Dudley into Angelsland, on their way to King Jaaz's Palace.

Angelsland felt similar to Leelaput. King Dudley was greeted by many folks who smiled and waved their hands, including Brickmaker, Teacher, Barber, and others. Children were playing in the back streets, aroma of delicious sweet pastries filled the air, and musicians could be heard, playing various instruments. Posters were displayed every hundred yards or so, with King Jaaz's picture, and each poster read: *We Love Our King*!

Yet, there were differences. Several years had passed since King Dudley's last visit, and he noticed some changes in Angelsland. All of the houses were well painted in a vast array of bright, pastel colors, and the roads were made of fine cobblestone. Leelaput's roads were made of dirt and gravel, and not all of the buildings were well painted.

King Dudley took note of how things had changed, but kept silent. Being a proud king, he was not very comfortable with the new, beautified Angelsland. Leelaput was clearly missing many of the fine things he saw in Angelsland, and hence, King Dudley felt bad about himself and his kingdom. Slowly, jealousy was creeping into King Dudley's heart. His mind wandered.

*So what if the houses are well painted and they have cobblestone roads? We can do that in our kingdom. We'll make even better roads than Angelsland's...*

"It feels a lot like Leelaput," said Pip.

"The roads are very nice," said Jordon, King Dudley's guard.

"We've had a lot of renovation lately. All the buildings are freshly painted and kept in good condition on King Jaaz's orders," said James.

"*We too* are in the process of renovating our kingdom," declared King Dudley.

As King Dudley noted the fine beautification of Angelsland, he felt less admirable because his own kingdom, Leelaput, was not as well kept. He exchanged a dialog with Jordon in an effort to prove to himself and the rest of the team that he was just as great a king as King Jaaz.

"Jordon, did you note the kind of cobblestone they've installed here?" asked the king.

"Yes, Your Majesty, it's very nice."

"Yes, but I think it is of a *lower quality* than the one we chose for *our kingdom* in our last governance assembly meeting. Isn't that right, Jordon?"

Jordon thought to himself quietly, *What governance assembly meeting was that? Hmm, I don't remember any such meeting.*

"You're absolutely correct, Dear King. In Leelaput, we are in the process of installing the very best possible cobblestone available, just as we discussed in our last governance assembly meeting."

Along the way, they saw beautiful water fountains, curb-side gardens, and government court buildings that were beautified with emblems made from solid gold.

As they approached the palace, the roads became less populous, and from atop their elephants, they could see a huge construction site where many men were working.

"Are they making large slides?" asked Pip.

James replied, "That's going to be a waterpark and

garden area for the people of Angelsland. The project will be finished in a few days, and King Jaaz has planned a grand opening ceremony."

"Wow! That will be so much fun!" exclaimed Pip.

The king turned to Jordon and requested, "Make note of that, Jordon! We've got to have that for our kingdom too!"

"Yes, Your Majesty," replied Jordon.

As they continued their journey forward, the party witnessed a grand spectacle unfolding very gradually before their astonished eyes!

Made of beautiful marble and pure gold, the monument emanated a heavenly splendor.

"What's that?" asked Pip.

"*That* is the King Jaaz's palace," said James.

"It's very nice," declared Pip.

Jordon observed King Dudley's uneasiness, and kept quiet. His face revealed anger and discomfort, and once again, his mind started to wander.

*That Jaaz has built a palace out of gold, Aye? He thinks he's better than the rest of us kings? We'll make an even better palace in Leelaput …*

King Dudley's party was greeted enthusiastically by King Jaaz. They sat in good cheer at a grand king's feast.

Dudley declared, "The last time I visited Angelsland, things looked very different. So I see you are very rich now, King Jaaz."

"I've always been rich, King Dudley. You see, even when the kingdom was not thriving as it is today, I've always had the *love* of *my people*. So I've *always* been rich. But today, I can afford a few nice things, and so I'm making the kingdom *just a little nicer*."

"Oh, I see, and *how exactly* were you able to make things, '*just a little nicer?*' Last time I visited you, *even your palace* was not well painted!"

"Oh, let's just say I found some buried treasure, *ha ha ha …*"

It was clear that King Jaaz did not want to reveal his secret as to where he was getting all of the gold from, but King Dudley was determined to find out.

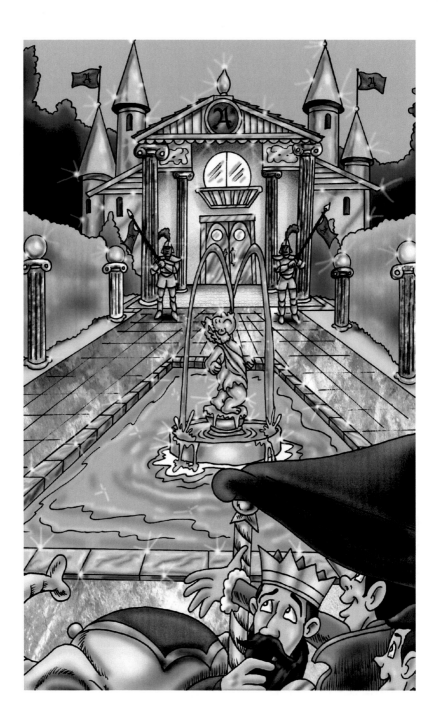

# CHAPTER 5

## Ambitious Dudley

**K**ing Dudley and his party were taken to guest quarters for the night. However, Dudley's jealousy had grown tremendously, and he could not sleep. His mind continued to echo the same jealous thoughts as before.

The next day, they prepared to return for Leelaput. Pip wanted to stay, hoping to enjoy the grand opening of the waterpark. King Jaaz pleaded for the guests to stay longer, but King Dudley was in *no mood* for enjoying *anything*.

As they left the kingdom, many people smiled and waved their hands at King Dudley's party. Dudley was uncomfortable, and didn't know what to do. He tried to smile back, and waved his hand uneasily, but his smile was fake.

"Close the curtains!" the king burst. The curtains of the platforms on top of the elephants where they sat were drawn, and they proceeded quietly out of Angelsland.

"He doesn't even have natural shade in his courtyard! *Our palace* in Leelaput does," babbled Dudley.

"Our palace is beautiful," said Pip.

"The service was so poor," the king added, "The food was not so tasty, and the sleeping mattress was *way too soft.*"

All of King Dudley's comrades felt that King Jaaz's hospitality was excellent, and thus, nobody had anything to say. Pip shrugged his shoulders, and couldn't understand his father's complaints either. Luckily, the king did not see.

All remained quiet while Dudley continued to fret, "*And that King Jaaz—who does he think he is*—building parks and a golden palace? Does he think he's better than the rest of us kings? He didn't even have the courtesy to come to my Fortieth birthday celebration!"

Many days passed, and the king's uneasiness grew.

One day, King Dudley approached his wife, Queen Isabella.

"Isabella, I'm a good king, aren't I?"

"Of course you are. Our people are very happy. You are a wonderful king!"

"Do you know what I saw in Angelsland? They've built cobblestone roads, gardens, a waterpark, and King Jaaz's palace is made of solid gold! Our kingdom doesn't have any of those things."

"*Solid gold?*"

"Yes, Isabella, solid gold."

Queen Isabella became very irritated and jealous on learning of King Jaaz's fortune.

"Well, we got to get the same things for our kingdom, especially a palace made of solid gold!"

"But we don't have enough money for that," the king said nervously.

"Find a way! You're the king!" replied Isabella, very adamantly.

"Yes, that's exactly what I was thinking."

A grand assembly was called to determine how to build a palace of gold, gardens, waterpark, and cobblestone roads in Leelaput. Based on the advice of his

top advisors, King Dudley decided to deploy a spy to settle into Angelsland, to figure out where King Jaaz was getting all of the gold from.

The assembly also concluded that in order to develop everything desired, the people of Leelaput would have to contribute by working much harder. Brickmaker was called into the assembly, and was questioned by the king's top advisor, Eby. After a lengthy inquiry, Eby devised a plan whereby Brickmaker and his wife could work twice as hard to make twice as many bricks, while selling the bricks at a slightly lower price to boost sales. Extra money made from the sale of the extra bricks would go towards paying for King Dudley's new golden palace.

"But I don't want my wife to work! She has so many other responsibilities!" pleaded Brickmaker. However, Dudley's new laws did not spare anyone. The same fate came to many others in the kingdom—Potmaker, Shoemaker, Pillowmaker, and others.

Barbers and teachers were not spared either. Their taxes went up, and some teachers were shifted to do manufacturing jobs, while the rest of the teachers took on twice as many students in their classes.

Meanwhile, the king deployed a spy to find out the

source of the gold. His name was Grayhound, and he settled into the heart of Angelsland, hiding very easily amongst the busy streets of the kingdom. He was a quiet, well-dressed man with keen eyes and a detective nature.

Grayhound kept a very close watch on the traffic coming in and out of King Jaaz's palace. It didn't take long to notice that every Friday morning, at about the same time, another young, well-dressed man came on horse carriage into the palace grounds.

He was a quiet and mysterious man, but dressed very much like Grayhound, and looked similar enough in appearance that one might mistake them to be brothers. Not knowing the man's name, Grayhound gave him the code-name of *"Friday,"* because he consistently came to King Jaaz's palace every Friday morning.

Grayhound was able to follow the horse carriage and noticed that after "Friday" left the palace, he made a stop at the brick factory of Angelsland, where bricks from the Angelsland's brick maker were loaded onto the carriage. Afterwards, the carriage stopped at the local pottery factory, where pots were also loaded onto the carriage. The carriage moved onwards from one

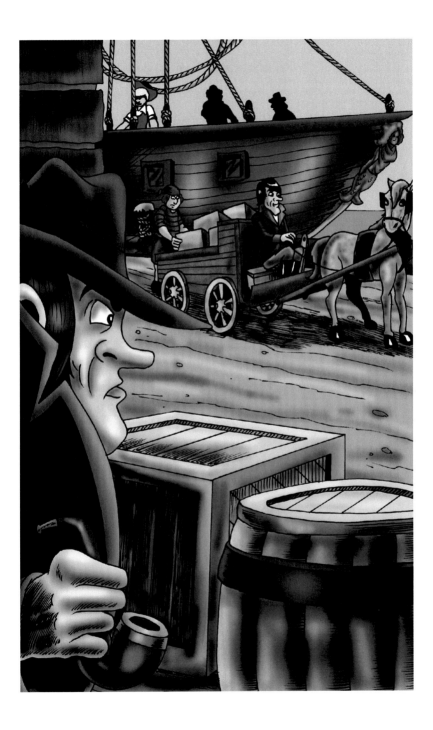

place to another, loading supplies of various kinds. Finally, "Friday" reached the ship port, and supplies from the horse carriage were loaded onto a ship. The horses were taken care of by a horse keeper at the dock, and the mysterious man disappeared aboard a ship with the merchandise every Friday afternoon. The ship returned the following Friday morning, and "Friday," the mysterious man, came out of the ship, and drove the empty horse-carriage back to King Jaaz's palace.

Grayhound returned to King Dudley and reported his findings. One day, King Dudley hired a ship to follow "Friday."

# CHAPTER 6

## Sneaking up on Jaaz

King Dudley, Jordon, and Grayhound rode Shirley to the dock, expecting her to climb aboard the vessel. The plan was to travel north, up the coast, and settle some place far away from "Friday's" ship, but close enough to keep a watch while following the ship. They were running out of time, and had to get there before "Friday's" ship would leave. But Shirley was afraid to get onboard, and wouldn't budge an inch closer to the vessel.

The king pleaded, "C'mon now, Shirley! Get on the vessel now. We gotta get going!"

But Shirley wouldn't listen. She was afraid, and Dudley's party grew increasingly impatient. They pulled her trunk, pushed with might on her bottom, but she still wouldn't budge!

Dudley cried in frustration, "Get on the vessel, you beast!"

Shirley made an angry elephant roar, "Roar!" Oh, she was angry! She sat down.

The king yelled out in frustration, looked at Grayhound and asked, *"Now what are we going to do?"* Grayhound didn't know how to solve that one.

Jordon had an idea. "Talk nicely to her, and give her something she likes," he said.

"Come on now, Shirley, I didn't mean it. You know I don't go anywhere without you, because you're my favorite elephant, and I love you!" the king pleaded.

The elephant got up! King Dudley and Jordon were amused and happy. "It worked!" exclaimed Jordon.

"C'mon now, Shirley! Get on the vessel now. We gotta get going!" said King Dudley. But Shirley wouldn't budge. She was afraid to get aboard.

Alas, a vicious circle! *"Any more bright ideas?"* asked Dudley.

"We got half of it. We talked nicely. Now let's offer her something she likes," said Jordon.

It just so happened that they were docked next to another ship that was loading sacks of roasted peanuts for export. Jordon was able to ask for a sack, and the trader was glad to help. Shirley trumpeted a beautiful elephant trump of great joy and excitement after tasting the peanuts from the king's hands.

"You can have the whole sack," Dudley said joyfully, as he lead a trail of roasted peanuts into the vessel, and left the sack on the deck.

They set out to sail, but not with ease. They appeared very silly, striving to sail through the waters, with the bulk of Shirley's weight on one end of the vessel. It appeared that Shirley's weight might sink the vessel! They were comically unaware of the situation. Jordon was the first to notice, and signaled a sign to King Dudley.

"Shirley! Get into the middle of the vessel!" Dudley shouted very angrily.

Shirley made an angry elephant roar, "Roar!" Oh, she was angry!

"Remember the rules," said Jordon, "Be nice and offer her something."

"Oh, I was just kidding, Shirley," said Dudley, "You

know you're my favorite elephant." He patted her big tummy, and put the sack of peanuts back to its original position—in the middle of the ship, and Shirley followed the sack.

Alas, they were set for a smooth ride!

After following "Friday's" ship, they found themselves off the coast of a tropical island.

It just so happened that on this particular Friday, King Jaaz also came aboard the vessel that sailed away from Angelsland with all the goods.

King Jaaz's ship landed onto the tropical island first, while King Dudley's ship snuck up from behind, at a distance. Jaaz's ship was unloaded, and goods from Angelsland were hauled away by tribal people, while King Jaaz set afoot inland to meet the tribal leader.

# CHAPTER 7

## Mystery Solved

Ookapa Island was a little-known, unexplored territory, and the tribal people spoke a different language. Upon landing, King Jaaz and "Friday" greeted the island's king, King Ookadady, and his ministers. Over the course of the year, Ookadady had learned English very well, because Jaaz had sent a teacher to learn Ookish from the Ooka people, and teach English to Ookadady and his ministers.

Meanwhile, King Dudley, Jordon, and Grayhound followed at a distance, very carefully, so as to not be noticed. Dudley's team had boarded Shirley, but they were striving to catch up with King Jaaz. Struggling to climb above the sand-dunes of Ookapa, Shirley was not comfortable with the terrain. Fortunately, King Jaaz and the tribal leader had started a lengthy dialog, and had no idea that Dudley's party was sneaking up from behind.

King Jaaz, "Friday," and Ookadady's people were not very far away, and King Dudley could see them clearly through his binoculars. Dudley saw that they were talking, but could not make out what they were saying.

Although Dudley could not hear what they were saying, Jaaz and Ookadady were exchanging words of continued friendship.

"Here's the last of the gold we have. The creek no longer contains all the gold it used to. There is hardly any gold left in it. I'm sad to see our trade come to an end, because we really like the kind of bricks and pottery you have brought us. But we have nothing to offer you in exchange."

"Don't worry, King Ookadady. Our friendship doesn't end here. I am going to send my best brick maker and best pot maker to Ookapa, and they will teach your people how to make bricks and pots in the style of Angelsland. Your people can also teach my craftsmen the unique design of Ooka bricks and pottery."

"You will do that for us?" asked Ookadady, in a tone that revealed much joy and thankfulness.

"Of course we will. You have my word!"

"You are very kind, King Jaaz!"

Jaaz burst in laughter, "Yes, I am… ha, ha, ha!"

"Cheers!" declared "Friday." They all had a friendly toast of fine drinks with good humor.

Finally, Ookadady handed Jaaz the final small pouch of gold.

It so happened that Dudley arrived at the scene right at that very moment!

"Ah ha! I caught you!" exclaimed Dudley.

Jaaz was startled to see his friend Dudley. They had an interesting exchange of words.

"Oh, King Dudley, what a pleasant surprise! *What on earth are you doing here?*"

"What am *I* doing here?" asked Dudley. "What am *I* doing here?" he repeated. "Shouldn't I be asking *you* that?"

Dudley stuttered, as he pointed his finger to the well-dressed man that they had code-named "Friday," "What are you and *this*—*this* man "Friday" doing here with these people?"

"*Friday?* His name isn't Friday! His name is Thursday!" replied Jaaz. By sheer coincidence, "Friday's" true name was Thursday!

"Don't try to get yourself out of this one! I know you've been trading with these people."

King Dudley looked at King Ookadady and asked, "*What's he giving you?* Whatever he's giving you, I'll give you twice as many bricks and pots for the same gold!"

"Actually, King Dudley, my trading contract with King Ookadady just ended today. That's why I came on an official trip to Ookapa Island to bid King Ookadady goodbye. But you're welcome to start a trading relationship with King Ookadady."

Just as Dudley was trying to comprehend everything, Jaaz kept talking, not giving him any time to think.

"Well, I've really got to be going now. King Ookadady, why don't you give King Dudley a tour of the stream where you're getting the gold from?"

That got Dudley very excited. Before Dudley could reply, Jaaz kept talking quickly, preparing to leave right away.

"Well, my dear queen is waiting, and we've got to make it back before dark. You know how it is driving the boat in the dark at night. Off we go!"

As Jaaz's party rushed away without a warm good-bye, Dudley thought to himself, *Oh forget him. Let's take a look at that stream full of gold!*

The two kings conversed as they walked to the special stream. Dudley's enthusiasm grew until he could no longer contain himself.

With joyful jubilation, King Dudley declared, "I'm sure my kingdom can have a great trading relationship with your people! Our bricks and pottery are of a higher quality than that of Anglesland."

They reached the stream.

"Wow! Is this where you're getting the gold from?"

"Yes, this is where gold used to be. But we can hardly find any left today. I gave the last of it to King Jaaz."

Dudley's face fell and his shoulders drooped as shock and disappointment overcame him.

"What do you mean—gave the *last* of it?"

"We used to find ten good nuggets every day, but today we're lucky if we find one in a month. For the last few months, we found nothing, but we had a stockpile of gold left over from last year's pan that we kept at my tribal assembly hall. But since King Jaaz was so much interested in the golden rocks, we just gave it to him."

King Dudley's jaw dropped in shock and horror.

"Ugh! That Jaaz! He's done it to me again!"

# CHAPTER 8

## The Trip Home

Of course, King Dudley was not happy as he left the island and headed back home.

To make matters worse, Shirley would not board the vessel—again!

"Quick! Where are the peanuts?" cried Dudley.

"She finished them," said Jordon.

"What do you mean, *she finished them*?" cried King Dudley, "Didn't you plan for the trip back?"

Jordon looked nervous and started mumbling. "Well. Aah. Um. It's like this, you see, Your Majesty," he mumbled, "Um. Aah, no sir, we didn't."

King Dudley reacted angrily, "Well, you've got to do better planning, Jordon! How many times must

I tell you, we can't do things hastily and whimsically! You've got to slow down, think carefully, and plan everything out before springing into action!"

"Sorry, Your Majesty," said Jordon.

"Sorry isn't enough! *Well, what are we supposed to do now?*" exclaimed Dudley.

Grayhound, being of a detective nature, observed that Shirley was making funny gestures with her trunk, almost as if she was sensing something; it appeared that she was scared to get on the deck for a good reason. He shifted his attention toward the deck. As he listened, he heard some strange noises.

"Shhh. Quiet. Listen. Do you hear the thumping sound?" interrupted Grayhound.

King Dudley and Jordon paused to listen carefully.

"It's coming from the deck," said Grayhound. "I think Shirley wants to go home too, but there's something on the deck that she's not comfortable with."

"Yes," declared the king, "Let's see what it is."

As they climbed aboard to investigate, lo and behold, they saw a bunch of mice whizzing to and fro! Shirley was afraid of mice.

"Ugh! Mice!" exclaimed King Dudley. "Quick!

We've got to do something! Grab something, and let's get them off this boat!"

The three men followed the king's orders and sprang into action. They picked up the first object that they could find and started chasing the mice. King Dudley grabbed a pot; Grayhound grabbed the empty peanut bag, while Jordon grabbed a broomstick and dustpan.

They were three silly men with objects in their hands, helplessly chasing mice back and forth. Each man ran to and fro, keeping his eyes on the deck, but not watching carefully where he was going. Running around helplessly and without success, they grew tired but continued to run, nonetheless. Exhausted, they all comically ran into each other, tumbling down on the ship's deck. There they were, on the deck—three silly men, with their hearts pounding, totally out of breath.

"*What are we doing?*" shouted the king.

"I think we're being hasty and whimsical, and we didn't do enough planning before we sprang into action," said Grayhound.

"Hey, that sounds familiar," replied Jordon. "Isn't that something we're not supposed to be doing?"

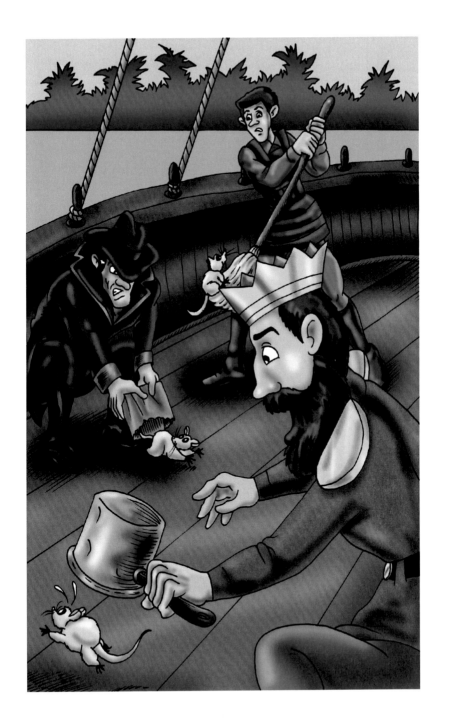

"*How are we ever going to get home with Shirley?*" panicked King Dudley.

Just then, Grayhound noticed a strange smell.

"Hey, do you smell that?" asked Grayhound.

"Yes. Its aged parmesan cheese. So what?" asked Dudley.

"Mice like cheese," replied Grayhound.

They went into the vessel's kitchen and found the cheese packet that the mice had broken into. Not all of the cheese was eaten; most of it was still left.

"Ah! I think I know where you're going," said Dudley.

They laid a wooden board connecting the boat to the shoreline, and created a trail of cheese that guided the mice down onto the shore. Shirley quickly climbed aboard into the boat after the mice ran out. They lifted the anchor and set sail, homeward bound, at last!

# CHAPTER 9

## From Misery to Hope

**m**any months passed. Strangely, Dudley remembered his good friend, King Jaaz, quite often.

"That Jaaz! Good for nothing friend! What did he ever do for me? How dare he show off his wealth with his gift to me! Couldn't even come to my party!"

Dudley rambled on and on, day and night, complaining about Jaaz.

Day by day, the king's jealousy became so ugly that he no longer could contain himself, and he started thinking ill thoughts against his friend.

*I hope his kingdom is ravaged by storms, and he suffers diseases from the fabled lands!*

One day, Dudley decided to step out of his palace, where he had miserably rooted himself for many months.

"Jordon!" shouted Dudley, "where are my royal shoes!"

Dudley was becoming very unpleasant to be around. Nobody in the palace liked his new communication style of shouting and complaining. Nevertheless, everybody obeyed the king without fail. Nobody liked him though. He was losing the love of his staff.

Jordon and Dudley stepped aboard Shirley, as they set out for a stroll in Leelaput. The streets of Leelaput no longer seemed lively, because people were working hard, on the king's orders, to create more wealth for the kingdom—wealth that was to be used for creating a new, golden palace for their king.

There were a few people on the streets, and they could see that their king was passing through. However, there were no smiles or friendly hand waves. The kingdom used to have many posters exclaiming the love of the people for their king, but most of those posters had withered away, and the few that remained were not in good condition.

"Jordon!" shouted the king, "Who's our poster maker? He's not doing a very good job of maintaining the posters!"

"We don't have any one poster maker, Your Majesty. Those posters are printed on a voluntary basis by each community of the kingdom. They are not required to keep the posters fresh," replied Jordon.

Jordon witnessed one poster that was almost withered away. The words, *We love,* were clearly crossed out. The words, *Our King,* remained on the poster. Jordon remained quiet, hoping that the king would not notice that poster. Luckily, he didn't. The people of Leelaput no longer loved their king. They were working hard to make him a golden palace and no longer had the luxury of time, nor the energy and enthusiasm for living happily.

"Well we shall have to enact a new law to keep posters up fresh all the time. Make note of that, Jordon!" exclaimed the king.

"Yes, Your Majesty," replied Jordon.

As they tread the dirt and gravel roads of Leelaput, the king suddenly remembered the roads of Anglesland.

"Jordon!" shouted Dudley. "Where are those cobblestone roads I ordered?"

Day by day, the king was not only losing his good humor, but also his memory.

"You ordered the assembly to buy gold for your palace, and we are still saving up for the palace," said Jordon.

"*Well*, when are you going to start *that* project?" asked Dudley.

"We have a bag of gold, but it isn't enough to build a golden palace."

"How many bags do you need?"

"We need about one hundred bags for a completely golden palace."

"*One hundred* bags? We need *one hundred* bags? Why didn't you tell me this earlier? We've got to do something!" exclaimed Dudley.

The king was shocked and angered. There was no way to build the golden palace quickly. It would take roughly twenty-five years to accumulate that much gold. Thus, the king prepared for a grand assembly to figure out how to generate more wealth quickly.

However, before the meeting could convene,

Leelaput was hit by a terrible storm, and the king was left to deal with major losses in his kingdom. The kingdom had major buildings, bridges, roads, and utility lines in need of repair. The added weight of these losses was too much for the king, and thus, he became ill.

The doctor came to see King Dudley one day, and it was reported that the king was suffering from unusual diseases called anxiety and hypertension. While such diseases were rumored to be common across the ocean within the countries of the fabled lands, in the continent of Kingsland, such diseases were highly unusual.

The fabled lands were outside the triangle, where ships dared not sail. The rest of the world outside the triangle was believed to belong to a different dimension. It was rumored that the ancestors of the current Kingsland residents had been sailors who had immigrated there from the fabled lands by penetrating through the triangle.

The king was not a very religious or spiritual person, however, he did have a spiritual advisor who was a fatherly figure to him during times of great need. The spiritual advisor was given the name of Wise-one by the many people whom had benefited from his guidance. A content and happy fellow, Wise-one's face always beamed with calm joy, peace, and good cheer.

"Oh, Wise-one, I'm so glad you're here!" exclaimed the king, "My health is failing, the kingdom is a mess, and my people no longer love me! Where have you been, Wise-one, and why didn't you come sooner?"

"You called me, and so I came. Why did you wait so long to call me?"

"Oh, you know how it is. A king's life is a busy life. *But what should I do now?*"

Wise-one had known all along of the problems that the king and his kingdom were facing—as well as the solution. But Wise-one was too wise to tell the king directly.

# CHAPTER 10

## Happy Days Again!

**W**ise-one asked, "You looked so happy on your birthday, so tell me, what happened since then?"

As Dudley explained his story to Wise-one, he traced back his steps, and came to a grand conclusion.

"Aha! Marvelous, Wise-one! Marvelous! All my problems started after I met King Jaaz on Oooka Island. That Jaaz! He's done it to me! He has cast an evil spell on me! And the kingdom is now in shambles, my health is failing, and everyone hates me. We should cast a spell back! And we should bring ruin to his kingdom!"

Wise-one remained calm, and gave a loving smile, full of compassion and understanding.

"No, my dear King Dudley. We should not wish such things. Such wishes bring about misery to the one who wishes them. Let's think this through a little more carefully. Would you want to build a golden castle today if you had never seen the one in Angelsland?"

The king thought for a moment, and answered, "No, I suppose I got the idea from Angelsland, and just want to make something better. The people of Angelsland love their king because he has a golden palace, and they beautified their kingdom. My people don't love me just yet, because we don't have all the things that Angelsland does."

"Most of your people haven't even seen Angelsland, nor do they know about Jaaz's palace. They loved you just fine before—so what has changed?"

"That Jaaz, he's cast a spell on me!"

"No, my dear friend, King Dudley. Think about the laws you introduced. The people are working very hard. They have no time to enjoy life. Go visit and talk with the people and see how they are feeling."

The king invited Potmaker, Brickmaker, and others into his palace.

"We just want things to be the way they were," Brickmaker stated.

"It would be nice to have cobblestone roads, a waterpark, and a golden palace, but not if we have to work so hard that there is no time for family, love, and happiness," said Potmaker.

The feelings of Potmaker and Brickmaker were warmly acknowledged by all the others.

"I think I understand," said the king.

After the guests had left, King Dudley continued his dialog with Wise-one.

"The people of your kingdom are tired and unhappy. They want to live as they did before with their benevolent king."

"I want to live happily as we did before too," the king said. "But *that Jaaz* has a golden palace, and I don't!"

Wise-one gave a calm, loving look to the king, and answered, "Do you remember what your friend Jaaz told you when you pointed out that he had become extremely rich?"

Dudley recalled, and then asked, "*How do you know about this? You weren't there.*"

It was common knowledge that Wise-one was endowed with visionary powers that allowed him to counsel people during difficult times. Yet the king

was always surprised when Wise-one demonstrated his powers.

"Yes, my dear friend, King Dudley, I come to know only of the needful through my visionary powers."

Dudley reflected on what Jaaz's reply had been.

*I've always been rich, King Dudley. You see, even when the kingdom was not thriving as it is today, I've always had the love of my people. So I've always been rich. But today, I can afford a few nice things, and so I'm making the kingdom just a little nicer.*

"Yes, I remember. Jaaz said that his richness was not his material wealth, but his richness was the exchange of love that he had with his people."

"You too are rich, because it's not too late. Repeal the new laws and let your people live happily. Make improvements that you would like to see in the kingdom that you are able to make comfortably, and enjoy the kingdom with your people."

"*But that Jaaz*! He tricked me, and left me nothing!"

"King Jaaz created a trading relationship with the Ooka people, because he was interested in their gold and the Ooka people were interested in Angelsland's bricks and pottery. If *you* had created such a trading relationship with the Ooka people, would *you* have volunteered to tell all of your friends about the gold?"

Dudley paused to think for a moment, and replied, "No, I guess… probably not. But why did he have to leave in such a hurry, knowing full well that Ookadady was leading me to a stream stripped of all gold!"

"He was uncomfortable because he sensed your jealousy. You rushed away from his palace when you saw how beautiful it was. Then in Ookapa, you snuck up on him from behind. King Jaaz could sense that you had an ambition to be greater than him."

"Yes! I want to be greater!" burst King Dudley.

"There is no end to comparison, King Dudley. There will always be people who have more than you, and there will always be people who have less than you. As far as greatness, it is not how much you have that makes you great, but it is how much love and friendship you and the people around you can experience that makes you great. As for richness, it is not what you have that makes you rich, but it is how you use what you have been given that makes you rich. Remember, you and your people were happy before.

The whole problem started when you began to compare yourself with King Jaaz and his kingdom."

King Dudley finally understood the solution to his problems. He felt as if a heavy load of bricks had been lifted off his back.

"I feel lighter and happier after talking with you—because now I know the solution to my problems. But still, I have a lingering question. Why have I always felt that I've never been such a good king? Even when the kingdom was happy, I always felt as if I were not quite so good as the people made me out to be."

"When the kingdom was happy, yes, you were a good king, my friend. Every time you lie, however, you are not only lying to people, but you are also lying to yourself. But you can't really lie to yourself, you see? In the back of your own mind, you will always know the real truth. In essence, you feel bad about yourself, because you know that you have lied to make yourself look good. And if you are constantly lying to make yourself look good, then how can you feel good about yourself? But think about why you lied. It has always been about pride. The people of Leelaput *don't really care* that you were unable to bring home the skin of a tiger. Cobblestone roads are nice to have. But be honest about it. There was no grand assembly, and you didn't pick any cobblestone for your kingdom. You got the idea from Angelsland. And if you really think about it, King Jaaz's palace and hospitality were very nice. You don't have to think badly about King Jaaz or his palace to feel good about yourself. All that your people want is a loving king—which you were, before you introduced those silly laws."

*"How did you know about all of those things? You weren't there."*

"I come to know of the needful, of course."

"Oh yes, by your powers. Well, Wise-one, I don't think I would know what to do without your help."

Wise-one smiled. "Yes my dear King Dudley, but I do recommend that you make things right with King Jaaz."

"I never wronged him!"

"Remember the rules: see no evil; hear no evil; speak no evil? But there is one rule that often gets missed. Do you know what it is?"

"I'm not sure."

"The last rule is: *think no evil.*"

King Dudley was embarrassed. "Yes. I wished some pretty bad things for my friend. But I don't think he would understand anything if I apologized to him. I might even make him uncomfortable by telling him the things that I was thinking."

"Then apologize in your heart and mind very humbly, and make a vow not to ever think such thoughts again."

Thus, King Dudley apologized in his heart and mind.

"There's still one thing I'm confused about," said

Dudley. "Thoughts seem to come automatically in my head. How do I make sure that the bad ones don't come in again?"

"Start paying more attention to what you are thinking—especially when you are not feeling good. Challenge what you are thinking."

"Wow, that's interesting. Anything else?"

"Yes. If you fill your mind up with creative and beautiful things, then the negative thoughts will tend to go away. You might listen to some nice music or read a comical book. You can even work to create something nice of your own, like a new park for your kingdom. But try to enjoy yourself, and don't be discouraged if you see a nicer park somewhere else. Enjoy what you have."

Thus, a grand assembly was declared at King Dudley's palace.

"Today, I declare the repealing of the *Work Like An Ox Act!*" exclaimed King Dudley. "And, I also declare that we will be using the money collected thus far very wisely."

"The heavy taxes that were so far collected are not going to be used for a golden castle. But we have just enough surplus to fix all the damages from the storms, build cobblestone roads, construct a waterpark, make gardens, and keep homes well painted within the kingdom. And that's exactly what we're going to do!"

The atmosphere was filled with wild cheers of joy and liberation!

"Glory to King Dudley!" cried the crowd.

The people of Leelaput were happy and relieved. They all looked forward to the construction of their new waterpark, although most people really didn't know what a waterpark was.

"Yay! We're going to make a waterpark!" exclaimed Mr. Baker.

"What's a waterpark?" asked Mrs. Baker.

"Don't be silly. It's a park with water in it."

"Oh yes, of course. Like a pond or fountain, right?"

"Yes, exactly!"

Fresh new posters went back up throughout the kingdom; the people's love for their king returned.

King Dudley also wanted to make relations better with his friend, King Jaaz. However, because Leelaput was facing many problems caused by the storms, King Dudley sent Messenger to King Jaaz, offering gifts

and good wishes for the Christmas season. But when Jaaz learned about the problems of Leelaput, he sent Angelsland's best engineers to assist in the cleanup efforts of Leelaput. Thus, friendship between the kingdoms was re-established.

Soon thereafter, Brickmaker came to visit King Dudley, his cousin, Queen Isabella, and his nephew, Pip, at the palace.

"Now that work has calmed down a bit, I'd love to see the tiger you hunted down in the jungle, King Dudley," said Brickmaker.

King Dudley blushed for a moment, but then remembered what Wise-one had told him.

Dudley spoke hesitantly, "Yes, well about the tiger, you see, there isn't one. It's a long story." King Dudley and Pip told their humorous and magical jungle adventure.

"Wow, that's an amazing story!" exclaimed Brickmaker.

"Every time I here that story, I get goose-bumps," declared Queen Isabella.

After a wholesome afternoon of story-telling and tea, Brickmaker left with a warm good-bye, and Pip commenced a dialog with his father.

"Father, why did you not lie about the tiger this time?"

"Well, it's like this, Pip. If I keep lying about myself, I won't feel very comfortable in the process, and in the end, I won't feel very good about myself either. Besides, it's like you said, Pip. The people of our kingdom *don't really care* whether we brought back home a tiger skin or not. They just want a loving king." Pip nodded his head.

"Now," Dudley continued eagerly, "Let's start thinking about the waterpark design."

Pip responded very excitedly, "Alright, Father! That sounds fantastic!"

The artist behind *King Dudley & The Golden Mystery* is John Mahomet, a cartoonist with over 40 years of experience in the entertainment industry, working for companies such as Warner Brothers, Disney, and Hanna-Barbera. No wonder the artwork is so good! Although available in eBook format, some people are delighted to showcase such a wonderful masterpiece in their home libraries.

*If you'd also like to order a physical copy of any King Dudley book for your home, order from*
**www.kamsbooks.com**

Next time you struggle with making a decision about what gift to buy someone, consider a King Dudley book!